ANNIE and SIMON

The Sneeze and Other Stories

ANNIE and SIMON

The Sneeze and Other Stories

Catharine O'Neill

CANDLEWICK PRESS

For Barry

First edition 2013

Library of Congress Cataloging-in-Publication Data

O'Neill, Catharine.
Annie and Simon : the sneeze and other stories / [Catharine O'Neill].—1st ed.
p. cm.
Summary: Recounts four adventures of Annie, her big brother Simon,
and their dog Hazel as they collect horse chestnuts, visit a lake to observe and sketch wildlife,
muse about the nature of dogs and cats, and deal with Simon's sneeze.
ISBN 978-0-7636-4921-0
[1. Brothers and sisters—Fiction. 2. Dogs—Fiction.] I. Title. II. Title: Annie and Simon,
the sneeze and other stories. III. Title: Sneeze and other stories.
PZ7.O5524Ans 2013
[E]—dc22   2011046618

13 14 15 16 17 18 SCP 10 9 8 7 6 5 4 3 2 1

Printed in Humen, Dongguan, China

This book was typeset in Berkeley
with hand lettering by the author-illustrator.
The illustrations were done in watercolor.

Candlewick Press
99 Dover Street
Somerville, Massachusetts 02144

visit us at www.candlewick.com

Contents

CHAPTER ONE

Living Things

One clear morning, Annie and Simon and Hazel the dog sat on the dock at Pickerel Lake.

Annie's big, big brother, Simon, looked through his binoculars.

"What are you looking for?" asked Annie.

"Anything," said Simon. "Any living thing. Want to have a look?"

"No, thanks, Simon. I have to make pictures."

Annie patted her paper. "I know what," she
said. "Whenever you find a living thing, I'll make
its picture."

"OK," said Simon. He picked up his binoculars
and looked up and down Pickerel Lake.

"Hey, hey, hey!" said Annie. "I saw a splash!"

"Where?" asked Simon.

"Right in front of us," said Annie.

Simon put down his binoculars. "I bet it was a fish," he said.

"I bet it was a frog," said Annie. "I like drawing frogs."

Annie picked up her crayon and scribbled a bit.

Simon looked at Annie's picture. "That's pretty froggy," said Simon, "but I think you need bends where the knees are."

Annie stopped scribbling. "Knees? Frogs with knees? Oh, Simon. Tee-hee. Tee-hee. Tee-hee-hee."

"Good grief," said Simon.

Annie put down her crayon. "Simon, we're going to help you look for living things. Come on, Hazel."

Annie and Hazel waded into the shallow water at the edge of Pickerel Lake.

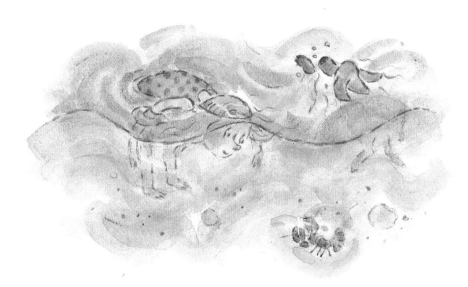

Annie stuck her head underwater and looked around. Then she popped back up. "Simon, Simon! I saw a little crayfish!"

"A crayfish," said Simon. "That's a living thing."

Annie ducked underwater again. Then she came back up. "There's a clam, too, Simon!"

"I'm coming in," said Simon.

"I'm coming out," said Annie. "I need to make pictures."

Simon waded in. He peered at the clam and the crayfish. "Good work, Annie," he said.

"And look," said Annie. "A dragonfly, too!"

Simon looked. "Oh, neat," he said.

Annie scribbled for a while. Then she showed Simon one of her pictures.

"The dragonfly," said Simon. "That's nice, Annie."

"It's the crayfish, Simon."

"Know what?" said Simon. "When a crayfish loses a claw fighting, a new one grows back in its place."

"Eek," said Annie. "That's strange."

Annie held up her next picture.

"A stone," said Simon. "That's good, too."

"It's the clam," said Annie.

"Guess what," said Simon. "It takes a clam one hour to travel this far." He held up his hands.

"Wow," said Annie. "That's slow."

Simon looked at Annie's last picture. "That must be the dragonfly," he said.

"That's what it is," said Annie.

"Here's something," said Simon. "A dragonfly can eat fifty mosquitoes in five minutes."

Annie put down her pictures. "Simon," she said, "do you know everything?"

"Well," said Simon, "I hate to brag."

Annie picked up her frog picture. "Maybe I
will put bends where the knees are," she said.

Annie scribbled a bit.

Simon and Hazel had a look.

"That's froggier," said Simon. "Definitely."

Annie laid her pictures out on the dock. "We've seen four whole living things, Simon."

"Pretty good," said Simon. "But hold still, Annie. I think I see a couple more."

Simon picked up a crayon and paper. Annie held still.

"Where are they, Simon? Are they bugs? Are they on me?"

Simon scribbled a little bit.

Then Annie and Hazel had a look.

"Tee-hee," said Annie.

CHAPTER TWO
The Sneeze

Annie and Hazel sat on Hazel's bed and looked at a book. Simon tapped on his computer.

"Hey, big brother," said Annie. "Want me to read you a story?"

"No," said Simon.

"It's really a good one," said Annie. "It's about an appendix."

"An appendix?" Simon sneezed. "Are you sure, Annie?"

"Yup," said Annie. "A little girl goes to the hospital because she's a sick person, and she has her appendix out and all her friends bring her flowers and want their appendixes out, too."

"Goodness," said Simon. He sneezed again.

"Hey," said Annie, "you're a sick person, too."

"I am not," said Simon.

Annie felt Simon's forehead. "Your forehead's all warm."

"That's a good sign," said Simon. "It means that I'm still alive."

"You're sick," said Annie, "and you neeed someone to take care of you."

"Uh-oh," said Simon.

Annie patted the sofa. "You lie down here, Simon, and stay resting. That's good for when you're sick."

"Well, why not?" said Simon. He lay down on the sofa. Annie fluffed up a cushion.

"This isn't so bad," said Simon. "Maybe I'll have that story now."

"Just a second," said Annie. "You need another thing for the sneeze."

Annie dragged a chair over to the hall tree.
"I can't reach my duck blanket, Simon. Can you
help me?"

"Sorry," said Simon. "I'm resting."

"It won't take very long," said Annie.

Simon got up and pulled down Annie's duck
blanket.

Annie wrapped the blanket around Simon's neck.

"There," she said. "Does that feel better?"

"It feels hotter," said Simon.

"You're supposed to be hot when you have a cold," said Annie.

"How about the appendix story now?" asked Simon.

"Wait," said Annie. "I need to get another thing."

Annie rummaged around in her toy box.

"Simon, can you dump all my stuff out for me?"

"Oh, brother," said Simon.

"I only need a little help," said Annie.

Simon got up and tipped everything out of Annie's toy box.

"There it is," said Annie. She handed Simon her violet hankie. "Here, I've hardly used it."

"I don't need a hankie, Annie. It's not that kind of sneeze."

"What kind of sneeze is it?"

"The tickly kind you don't need a hankie for," said Simon.

"Still," said Annie.

Simon lay down again.

"I know one more thing you need," said Annie. "Gummy bears. Especially the orange ones."

"I like the red ones, too," said Simon.

Annie looked behind some books on the shelf.

"Hey, my gummy bears fell down the back."

"Now you're going to want me to get up and reach them for you," said Simon.

"No," said Annie. "I can reach them."

Annie held up the bag of gummy bears.
"That's funny," she said. "They're all stuck
together. And the orange ones are all gone."

"Maybe you need a better place to hide them,"
said Simon. He tickled Hazel's tummy.

"I think I can pull you off some," said Annie.

"That would be good," said Simon.

Annie patted her big brother's nose. "How's your sneeze, Simon?"

"Fine," said Simon. "Just fine. Now will you read me the appendix story?"

"Oh," said Annie, "you're going to like it!"

Annie and Simon and Hazel snuggled under the duck blanket.

Annie opened her book.

"Guess what, Simon. I can't really read yet."

"That is true," said Simon.

"Will you read me the appendix story?" asked Annie.

"Of course," said Simon.

CHAPTER THREE

Hazel, Hazel, Hazel

Hazel hunted in the grass for bugs. Annie tapped on Simon in the hammock.

"Knock, knock, Simon. Want to see my new pictures?"

"OK," said Simon, "as soon as I finish my book."

"How many more pages are there?" asked Annie.

"Hold on." Simon checked. "Three hundred and six."

"Hey, you're teasing," said Annie. "No fair."

Annie spread her pictures on the grass.

Simon stuck his head out of the hammock.

"Are those all Hazel pictures, Annie?"

"Yes," said Annie. "Just Hazel, Hazel, Hazel.
Because she's so cute."

"Hmm," said Simon.

"This one's Hazel sleeping," said Annie. "And this one's Hazel sleeping. Here's Hazel sleep— Hey! There's Gray Cat from Next Door."

Annie patted Gray Cat's stripy tail.

Hazel hid behind a tree.

"I love cats," said Annie, "because they purr.

Like this. Mm-mmm, mm-mmm, mm-mmm."

Hazel began to bark.

Annie sighed. "If only Hazel were a cat, then she could purr, too."

"That's not all," said Simon. "She could meow. And climb trees. And puff up when she's mad."

"Wow," said Annie. Gray Cat twitched his tail. Hazel barked harder.

"Of course," said Annie, "I'm happy Hazel is a dog. Even if she can't purr."

Suddenly Gray Cat scooted under the bushes. "What's Gray Cat doing in there?" asked Annie.

"Cat things," said Simon. He settled back into the hammock and opened his book.

"Only three hundred and two pages to go," he said.

Everything was quiet for a while . . . except for now and then an odd noise.

"What's that sound?" asked Simon.

"It's Hazel," said Annie. "I'm teaching her to purr."

"Holy mackerel," said Simon.

"Want to hear?" asked Annie.

Simon climbed down. He put his ear next to
Hazel.

"First I scratch Hazel's chin a bit," said Annie.
"Then I squeeze her, but not too hard. Like this."

Hazel made a noise. "Urrgh."

"That's Hazel purring!" said Annie. "There! Hazel
the Purring Dog! Doesn't that sound nice?"

Simon crossed his arms. "It sounded more like Hazel the Grumbling Dog to me," he said.

"Grumbling?" said Annie. "It did not! Huh!"

Hazel went back to barking.

"Look," said Simon. "There goes Gray Cat."

"What's he got in his mouth?" asked Annie.

"Uh," said Simon, "it looks like a mouse. . . ."

"A mouse!" said Annie. "Gray Cat kills things? AAAGH!"

"I think it's called hunting," said Simon.

Gray Cat took his mouse next door.

"Hazel snaps at flies," said Annie, "but she never gets any!" Annie gave Hazel a hug. "Oh, Hazel, Hazel, Hazel. I don't mind if you can't purr."

Simon climbed back into the hammock and
opened his book. "Hey," he said, "I've lost my page."

"It was hundreds from the end," said Annie.

Simon hunted for his page. "What if we call
her Hazel the Fly-Snapping, Mouse-Fearing Dog
Who Says Urrgh?"

"I think she's just Hazel, Hazel, Hazel the Dog," said Annie.

"Oh, that's nice," said Simon. He settled in to read.

Hazel rolled over onto her back and waved her legs around.

"Simon, Simon, Simon," said Annie. "Look what Hazel's doing now!"

"What? What's she doing now?"

"Dog things," said Annie. "She's so cute."

Simon stuck his head out of the hammock. "She is pretty cute," he said.

CHAPTER FOUR

Horse Chestnuts

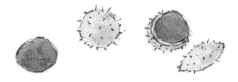

Annie and Hazel rolled home from the music shop in the green wagon. Simon led the way.

"Hang on to my new guitar string, Annie."

"I am hanging on, Simon. HEY!" The wagon went over a bump. "This is fun," said Annie. "I love summer. I think I love summer the best."

"Maybe you do," said Simon, "but summer ended three days ago. It's fall now, Annie."

"Fall," said Annie. "Really, Simon? Then maybe
I love fall the best."

Simon pulled the wagon past the park.

"Look," said Annie. "Nuts everywhere!"

"Neat!" said Simon. "Horse chestnuts."

"Let's take them home, Simon. Ouch!"

"I'll get the prickly ones, Annie."

Simon helped Annie fill the wagon with nuts.

Annie helped Simon pull the wagon home and carry it onto the porch.

"Can we eat the horse chestnuts now, Simon?"

"Nope," said Simon. "Only squirrels can eat horse chestnuts, Annie."

"But what about horses?" asked Annie.

"Horses?" said Simon. "I don't know about horses."

Annie and Hazel and Simon went inside and sat at the kitchen table.

"Here's your new guitar string, Simon. I'm hungry."

"Thank you," said Simon. "Have a banana."

Simon unwound the old string from its peg.

Annie peeled her banana and she looked out the window.

"Simon, there's a squirrel in the garden."

"What do you know," said Simon.

"It's got a nut in its mouth," said Annie.
"It looks like a horse chestnut."

"You don't say," said Simon. He tried to
wind the new string onto its peg. "Grrr."

"The squirrel's digging a hole," said Annie.
"Now it's dropped the nut into the hole."

"This winter," said Simon, "that squirrel will dig under the snow and eat the nut for dinner."

"It'll be all muddy," said Annie.

"Squirrels don't mind," said Simon. "Grrr."

"The squirrel's back with another nut, Simon."

Annie made Hazel a banana-peel hat.

"Here's the squirrel again, Simon! That's three whole nuts. Let's go get ours."

Annie ran to the porch. Hazel came, too. The green wagon was empty.

"Hey!" said Annie. "Our horse chestnuts are all gone!"

Simon stuck his head around the door. "Uh-oh. I wondered where all those nuts were coming from."

Annie sat down on the top step. Hazel sat down, too. "Oh, bad squirrel!" said Annie.

"What a thing," said Simon, and he sat down, too. "One squirrel burying all those nuts so fast."

Simon fiddled with his guitar string. Annie wiggled Hazel's ears. Everyone thought about the missing nuts.

"Maybe it was a gang of squirrels," said Annie. "What do you think, Hazel?"

Hazel gave her ears a shake.
She waved her nose this
way and that.

Then she sniffed

inside the green wagon.

She sniffed around the porch.

She sniffed down every step.

When Hazel reached the bottom, she wagged
her tail and dove under the big fern.

Annie poked her nose under the big fern, too.
"Simon, it's the horse chestnuts! Hazel found them!"

Simon came to see. "Excellent!" he said.

"But who put the nuts here?" asked Annie.

"Maybe the squirrel didn't want other squirrels to steal the nuts in the wagon," said Simon.

"Oh," said Annie. "So it hid them as fast as it could under the fern."

"Now it's burying them one by one in the garden, where they will be safe for the winter," said Simon.

"That's so clever," said Annie. "And now we can take them all back."

Simon raised his eyebrows.

Annie frowned. "I guess we could leave the squirrel a couple of nuts, Simon."

"A couple's something," said Simon.

"Or maybe half," Annie said.

"Half would be nice," he said. Simon plucked his sweet new guitar string.

Annie looked at the horse chestnuts again. Then she picked out three nuts. "Here, Simon. One nut for you, one nut for me, and one nut for Hazel. The squirrel can keep all the rest."

Simon gave Annie a kiss on the top of her head. "You know," he said, "you're my favorite little sister."

"I know," said Annie.